What's **BIGGER** than a digger?
BIGGER than a dinosaur?

DIGGERSAURS ARE BIGGER!

Turn the page and find out more!

Diggersaurs dig with bites so BIG,

CHOMP!!

WHOOPS!

each SCOOP creates a crater . . . .

They're **TOUGH** and **STRONG**

With cheery smiles
they **DUMP** huge piles

of rubble off their backs . . .

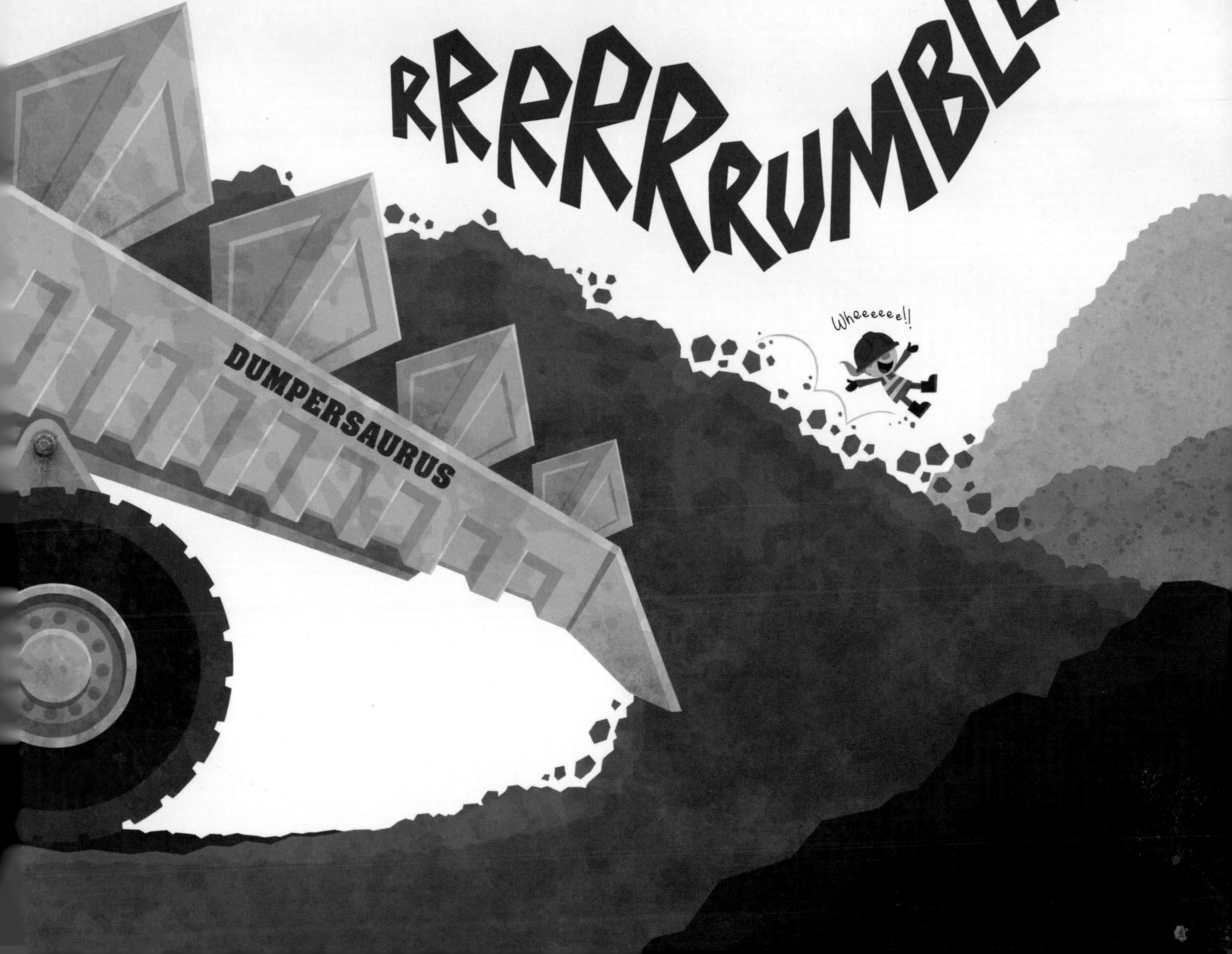

They shake around
and BREAK the ground –

their favourite ones are rusty!

They really love
to push and
SHOVE

MASSIVE mounds of rocks . . .

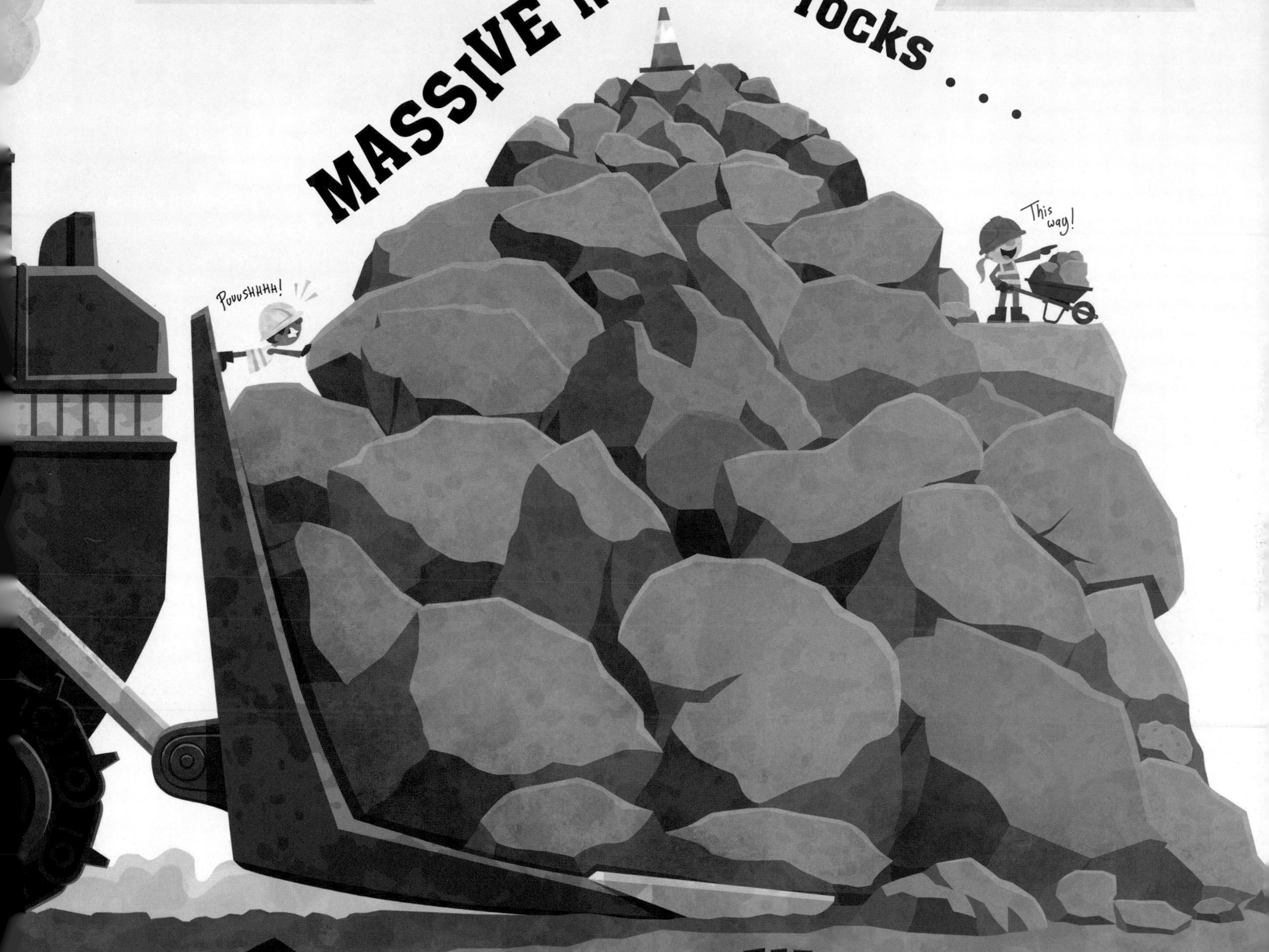

SCRAAAAPE!!!

and build tall tower blocks!

With spiky scales

DRILLERSAURUS 9

WHIRRRRRRRRRRRRRRRR!!!
and pointy tails
they spin and DRILL deep holes . . .
What's this?!

TOOT TOOT!!

There won't be lumps or humps or bumps

wherever this one ROLLS!

This one feeds on plants and weeds,

Nom-Nom!

and mows the grass so GREEN . . .

This one's beeping, brushing, **SWEEPING,**

keeping all things clean!

BEEP
BEEP!

SWEEPERSAURUS

12

WHOOPS!

All together – hear them
ROAR!

For Sophie

PUFFIN BOOKS

UK | USA | Canada | Ireland | Australia
India | New Zealand | South Africa

Puffin Books is part of the Penguin Random House group of companies
whose addresses can be found at global.penguinrandomhouse.com.

www.penguin.co.uk   www.puffin.co.uk   www.ladybird.co.uk

Penguin
Random House
UK

First published 2017
014

Copyright © Michael Whaite, 2017
The moral right of the author has been asserted

Printed in China
A CIP catalogue record for this book is available from the British Library

ISBN: 978-0-141-37550-2

All correspondence to:
Penguin Random House UK, One Embassy Gardens, 8 Viaduct Gardens, London SW11 7BW